CARNIVALIA

CARNIVALIA

Glenn Shaheen

GOLD WAKE

CONTENTS

For Laurie

TWO ACTORS

Two actors are shooting a scene in which they must act as though they are arguing while moving a couch. The argument stems from a romantic failure, some scraping lace from years before, when they were young. The two actors in the scene, playing the characters who are arguing, similarly had a romantic failure when they were younger, but it wasn't anything big, and they have stayed friends in the years since. The characters' argument is exasperated by the difficulty of moving such a heavy couch. The actors, in their capacity as actors, must act as though they are moving a very heavy couch. The first couch, fake and with Styrofoam where wooden beams would go to make it lighter, had earlier been nixed by the director in favor of a legitimately heavy couch that catches the late afternoon sunlight on its orange fabric more vibrantly. The script calls for the characters to struggle as they move this couch out of a small door, and the actors struggle as they move the couch in the staged scene. The characters, in their capacity as fictional ex-lovers, only move the couch once, have only one argument. The actors must do three takes, each time fake arguing while moving the couch from the fake living room through the fake door again, although two PAs reset the couch to its original location each time. When the first actor gets home after the day's shooting is over, he is in pain. He is sweat-soaked. His wife asks what the scene was about, what was so difficult about the day. He says it was about heartbreak. The second actor goes home in solitude.

KING LEAR

I didn't think it was a better time, the 90s, my teenage years all homemade fire and explosives. My friend's mom was a crack addict, we knew it and he joked about it, but that meant we could go to his trailer home and its large acres of woods and shoot guns, make bombs and see who'd stand closest. None of us was hurt by shrapnel or errant flame. Kids now, I don't get them, they tell stories of trying out meth or setting their brothers' feet on fire and I'm disgusted. Do they tell it with a different language? Is the clef all broken, lines turning into a child's scribbles as the notes dribble off? My friends tried meth, it was a curio. When Lisa described it to us, she said she wanted to clean her house for 24 hours and we thought it was cool, maybe we'd do it if time or opportunity emerged from the curtained shadows, which for most of us did not happen. Once my friend bought an AK-47 from a gun show, legally, and we shot it in the woods. A neighbor called the cops with a noise complaint, and when the officer saw a bunch of white kids (I was white before 9/11) with a gun made famous by movies and video games, he joined us in awe, shot a couple rounds himself. Kids these days don't talk about guns, don't talk about bombs, as if to mention them would make them manifest physically—Bloody Mary in the mirror. In the 90s we had such a purse between us Americans, wealth and the idea of endlessness. We were sure the next generation of reckless teens wouldn't have our racial problems that we laughed nervously about, our homophobia. I was an atheist and I made sure everybody knew it, made an inverted cross out of beads and leather to hang around my neck. I would hide it in my bag once I got off the bus so my parents wouldn't see me needling the locals.

Kids these days, I want them to avoid the suffering we knew, but the language is already in them. We thought America was a joke, they wear flag pins on their lapels and get nervous when somebody questions the legitimacy of extranational actions in class. Begin all doubts with "I love America, but…" When Clinton was getting blown, my friends and I were fumbling in the dark, girls and boys and all the ways we failed to fit together. Ken Starr's report was hot stuff.

Iraq fucked us up, the border of our youth even when I didn't go (though I tried to go to spite my mother, my eyes were deemed way too bad). Adam got his shins shredded on a road patrol, is now on antipsychotics. Derrick lost hearing in one ear because of an IED, posts his Purple Heart on the wall. My brother had a rocket explode in front of him, speaks sad nonsense in his sleep. Not to mention the people they surely had to kill, the people they won't even mention. Stories that could unfold like all the best failed trips and drug experiments we used to trade. I hope the companies who rented the American Brand for those years do well, the infrastructure dealings, commercial spots on War News, and oil. Kids now, they'd do it because of duty? Is that what they believe? What industry will push them into acting valorously, children who reenact the climaxes of action movies produced to demonstrate sacrifice and honor by corporations with mouths to fill with the best steak? Winter, we tell them it seems endless this year. Then it is summer, which is also endless.

THE FUTURE SUICIDES

Terry and Jada met in group therapy for people who survived a suicide attempt. They quickly bonded, both being twenty-somethings in love with 90s indie music and the Seattle scene, because they both used the same method when they tried to kill themselves (pills). They decided to start a grunge band, The Future Suicides. Terry played bass, and Jada sang and played rhythm guitar. They needed a drummer, so they put up flyers. "Drummer? Like The Screaming Trees or Mudhoney? Attempted or seriously contemplated killing yourself? Call Jada or Terry!" Soon Darwa joined the group. She was a bad drummer, but that was kind of the point. They wrote some messed up chunky songs and recorded them on an old style cassette 4-Track. They began to get some gigs around town and get a name for themselves. Soon, though, Jada successfully killed herself, shortly before The Future Suicides played their first travel show. Terry and Darwa scrambled to replace her, someone who could learn the songs quickly. They found Gil, and people didn't mind that Gil's voice was much lower than Jada's, the travel show was sweaty and energetic. Darwa killed herself a few months later, right after they booked some time in a studio. Again, they weren't great musicians, so it wasn't that hard to replace Darwa on drums, but Terry didn't take it so well, even if Penny was classically trained (and of course, like it even had to be mentioned, had tried to commit suicide when she was in middle school). The Future Suicides were getting big, as much for their commitment to early 90s grunge/noise as for their dedication to their mission statement. It's not an easy world to stumble through, and nobody likes someone who pretends it is. Terry felt obligated, even though the band was doing well, was getting so much acclaim in such a short time, to try to kill himself again, and he, too, succeeded. Replacing the bass player of the band was the least difficult of all. People referred still to the band as The Future Suicides. An idea more than people. A nation amidst the current. Stark cries in the waning light.

MILK

I keep finding medium length blond hairs on old shirts I haven't worn in two or three years. My hair is short and black, and my lover's hair is long and brown. I mention the hair to my lover, in idle passing, the general sort of banal logorrhea that tumbles out of the mouth. My lover jokes that the hair was an ex's, that I should wash my shirts more often. We laugh, but I have never dated anybody with medium length blond hair, or any length blond hair, although it has been pointed out that I have a tough time discerning what blond really is. I think, for example, that Marie, our friend from Idaho, has light brown hair, but my lover says it is clearly blond hair, that I must be joking. I can tell when very blond hair is blond, definitively yellowish or almost white, but the borderline hair, the dirty blondes, are fuzzy to me, like some greens, blues, and turquoises. They run together, and when a group of four or five people including my lover all say that I'm wrong and the shirt is definitively blue, that the woman is definitively blond, I get uncomfortable, I feel like I'm passing out, the part of a dream where you know it's a dream but are still paralyzed by terror, cannot move, cannot cry for help. I feel the tethers of the world around me, and yet I know, as I age, that more and more of them become severed. The blond hairs show up on more shirts, even tangled around my clean underwear. We make tortilla soup and I pull a cheesy hair out of my mouth, blond. Who was this person? Could I have loved some blond-haired woman with a medium length cut and forgotten about it? I visited home recently, and my brothers and sisters recounted the time I found a bat and tried to nurse it back to health. I don't remember any of it. A sewage pipe in our house had broken and our cellar was flooded with stench. A bat made its way to our kitchen, and I caught him, I placed him in a jar with some milk. My intentions seemed good, I don't know—the bat drowned in the milk. It was weak and fell face first into the milk and drowned. My brothers and sisters laughed, they said I was distraught and it sounds like a sad story but it's only pictures in my mind. I see myself from the outside, a kid in a blue shirt, holding a jar up to the light.

ENTERPRISE

A friend of ours got called up to the major league, so we wanted to see him play. We were going to buy tickets, but he told us he could get us family/friends seats, but they wouldn't be that good. That was fine with us—we were probably going to have to get nosebleed seats on our own anyway. Then at the last minute a rich friend gave us two of his club seats. We walked into a special room where they eyed us with anger until we showed our tickets, and then we were honored guests. I only wanted a hot dog, but they had a full all-access buffet. We ate very little, we were shy, and went out to our seats, which were behind the mound. A few seats away was an elderly former president and his wife. They stayed through the seventh inning, and then left, the president in a wheelchair. A friend later said I should have said something, criticized the man, but he was president decades ago, and I was a kid. What is a president but a figure built for anger. Now he struggles to walk to his wheelchair. At home, I've got headphones on, I am listening to Danger. The beats are aggressive and European. My father watched the baseball game because we could be seen on television every few minutes. Our friend went up to pinch hit once and flew out. Throughout the game, servers kept asking what we needed, what we wanted, but we always said, nothing, thank you, there's nothing we need.

NICE TWITTER

I was applying for jobs so I had to make my Twitter feed nice. That meant no saying "fuck," obviously, and probably fewer instances of calling the St. Louis Cardinals the St. Poois Shartinals, but mostly it meant stepping out of political debates. My father says to me "Now Jeff, you know when you put something on the World Wide Web then anybody can see it, and you don't know who that anybody may be." He says this to me after I criticize Israel's latest bombing of Palestine on my Twitter and Facebook. I never said "Fuck Israel" or anything like that, I just posted a link that discussed the murdered Palestinian children, and I said Israel needed to be sanctioned for its actions. I kept tweeting and retweeting things critical of the Israeli campaign which seemed deserving of internet criticism from some stranger thousands of miles away. All the pictures of dead kids kept getting to me, and part of it was that the dead kids looked like me, yes, but to be honest, many of the Israeli soldiers also looked like me, which bothered me as well, to think that maybe some version of me could be cajoled by rhetoric into shooting an unarmed child or dropping a bomb on a playground. A couple of my college friends who were (apparently) extremely pro-Israel unfollowed me. That's the only way we kept in touch, so did that mean they decided we were never going to be actual friends again? Around this time I read a story about a professor who got fired for his tweets about Israel. The college world is supposed to be leftist, supposed to be progressive, and I was in the process of applying for jobs in academia. My twitter feed was just politics, Batman, the Milwaukee Brewers and jokes. I tried to stop saying curse words, to stop criticizing in-power political regimes, but injustices kept happening. I couldn't not engage, but my fear of not being hired, of not getting a job, made me tweet vague remarks like "It sure is a tragic world." and "I hope all children get a chance to grow up." It wasn't helping, it sounded like stuff a racist uncle would say to excuse police shootings or systematic oppressions. What difference did my tweets make one way or the other? I wasn't getting interviews, and all my mentors and friends said it was astonishing I wasn't getting interviews. I never deleted my old tweets, true, but there were so many nonsense baseball tweets since then that I doubt anybody was coming up on my pro-Palestine internet self and saying "Let's put this radical bozo in the no pile." In college at a touch football game, a friend wore an IDF shirt and said we never trash-talked enough at our football games, so I asked him if he brought a machine gun to shoot me whenever I make a great catch. He didn't think that was very funny. It was a couple months after 9/11 and none of my friends liked it when I mentioned being Arab anymore, they thought I was just trying to get pity points. A truck full of rednecks followed me home one night and yelled "Arab!" out the window at me, but it *was* rural Georgia—that's the kind of thing that could have happened before 9/11 to be honest. I went to join the Arab-American student union on campus, but I was one of only two people there who didn't speak any Arabic whatsoever. When I told the group's president how I grew up saying grandmother, he said it definitely was not an Arabic word. It felt like my grandmother never even existed. My parents called that year and told me it was as good a time as any, in that new scarred America, to shave my beard and tell people my name was Danish or Gaelic, to wear an American flag shirt. I could have erased my Arab self! Many people would think that's a poisonous thought, but there have been many times in which I regret not hitting that shuffle button, just stumbling through the rest of my life as a swarthy white dude. People would still ask me what I am, but I could just puff my chest out and say "Welsh-Irish," and everybody in the room would quiver a little. I could have been so white I became unknowable. I could have been comfortable crushed into that background.

CIVILIZATION

You boil eggs. You twirl keys. You live bells. You peel grapes. You run slow. You watch art. You map hives. You sog gloves. You harm time. You out side. You slam books. You drink slow. You figure out. You walled in. You pound street. You hear bells. You climb stairs. You station cross. You fake sick. You tear page. You halve bread. You cloud thoughts. You rib cage. You free bird. You strep throat. You clean plate. You scar magenta. You break dolls. You shelve books. You menace kids. You call mom. You call me. You twist phone. You palm coins. You trash trash. You lay slow. You light house. You fill rooms. You walled in. You flit quick. You lay flat. You let ring. You cold heart. You face glass. You real tooth. You fake feather. You lovely lovely. You spin tops. You sip bells. You pen note. You place shoes. You hard time. You eat fruits. You sleep well. You plate delicately. You file note. You drink slow. You lose two. You tongue silver. You sack fruits. You boil tea. You signed leaf. You stag none. You miss lovely. You bell slow. You fear light. You out side.

INFINITE PALACE

The Infinite Palace must also contain infinite dungeons. In the infinite dungeons are, of course, an infinite number of prisoners, experiencing an infinite amount of pain. Their crimes are infinite, yes, but there is also an infinite number of people who are guilty of no crime and tortured anyway, infinitely. Infinite skins punctured by infinite iron maidens, infinite meals held just out of an infinite reach. The infinite dungeons of the Infinite Palace are the darkest place in the universe, with an infinite amount of shadow and misery, yet the infinite number of small cracks in the infinite bricks let in an infinite amount of light and hope. Because of this, the infinite dungeons are also the brightest place in the universe. To be held in the infinite dungeons, or even to visit, briefly, is to learn the degree to which we will accept the suffering of others if it means that we are not the ones enmeshed in pain's river. Two ivory statues of saints guard the entry to the dungeons, both covering their faces in their hands. What majestic creatures were killed for this minor aesthetic detail?

THE DRONE

In college, a girl I liked, Erin, came to spend the night for a Le Tigre concert and I begged her to take care of a huge cockroach that found its way into the living room. I realized it would mean our relationship would only continue in a platonic sense from then on, but I just needed it gone, I couldn't take it darting around. I knew it would find its way onto my face in the night and that would be it, my brain would just shut off. So she killed the roach and it was over, I was fine with it. My brain knew I would find another woman to fall for some day, and maybe no cockroach would ever come into my house ever again. Some apartments just seemed to attract more roaches, and others I would live in for years without ever having one roach. It was only palmetto bugs that seriously bothered me, the flying ones. Even though the smaller roaches, German cockroaches, were worse, signaled infestation, the one time I had a place with those bugs, it didn't bother me that much. They were plentiful, but small. I could kill them and it didn't make me feel too terrible. That was my main problem, that I could not bring myself to kill big cockroaches, no matter how much I hated them. Their size crossed a boundary for me—as big as a mammal, a mouse, and I could imagine their suffering. I could imbue them too easily with human characteristics. Spraying them with poison, watching them writhe in agony as their nervous system boiled away was more than I could handle. And crushing them—they had guts, and their splintered carapace mixed with the tapioca goo reminded me of jpegs college friends would shock me with of shattered human bodies from building missteps or serious car accidents. My friends liked that seeing death would ruin my night. I couldn't stop talking about the mangled

16

bodies they showed me, and sometimes I'd cry, which made them laugh hardest. I got a cat after college, and unluckily found my way into another apartment with really old plumbing that palmetto bugs would use to get into the sink or tub. What was lucky though is that my new cat would grab the roaches as soon as he saw them, shove them into his mouth without hesitation and eat them. I'd have to plug my ears so I didn't hear him crunch them up, so I didn't imagine the burn of hopeless adrenaline that I would feel trapped between the teeth of a tiger. The cat eating them was part of the "circle of life," I'd tell myself, my guests. I eat meat, but not candy or cookies shaped like people or animals. I never throw out any toy or doll with a face. On MSNBC's homepage there was a story about a drone being shot down over Pakistan. The picture of the sad, crashed drone, its crumpled wings stuck broken at acute angles, looked like a bird I hit years ago with my car. It sat suffering on the side of the road, breathing syncopated as it died, and I could not bring myself to put it out of its misery even though my father said it was the most humane thing to do.

CORIOLANUS

My wife has starting smoking. Well, she began to smoke in high school, everybody did really, but she has now started to smoke for real. She buys packs on a regular basis. The clerk at the Snapy Snacky knows her brand and everything. I tried to tell her to stop, that she would die much sooner if she didn't, but that's no argument. Neither of us wants to live to see the other die. I have high blood pressure, so I've already got a decade or so advantage over her. Tobacco is a resilient crop, and it is doing fine. There have been food riots lately; many of the chemicals used to make potato chips, candy, junk food, and fast food burgers have been in extreme shortage all year. There is not a food shortage, no—just a chemical shortage. Crops are abundant. We have to eat leafy greens almost every meal and fresh eggs. It's too much for many to handle. They want their frozen Boneless Wyngz* (*no real wing meat) with flavor dustings of all shades of salt. Tobacco is a leaf, it is untouched and my wife puffs away. Puff puff. I become healthier and healthier, I can't avoid it. My doctor says my blood pressure is that of a very fit senior citizen, which is a decent start for me. I make a terrific sandwich with cucumber and arugula paste and worry I'll live until I'm 90. On a business flight I sit next to an older woman. Outside the plane are two layers of clouds. They look like frozen ocean waves. The sun makes a single diagonal beam that cuts the scene, and I must bother the stranger, the older woman. She looks up from her book and she is crying. I apologize, I hesitate. I say there is something beautiful outside and she nods, says thank you, and turns back to her book.

PAPER DOLLS

Television shows about people fighting and television shows about the malls of the world and television shows about specific wartime atrocities and television shows about the best methods for maintaining a beehive and television shows about murder of course and television shows about white people with white friends and television shows about nudity on parade and television shows about noble recovery from college heroin addiction and television shows about the making of television shows and television shows about a desert and soda machine and television shows about mincemeat not being meat and television shows about animals in deserted alleyways eating from cardboard boxes and television shows about coining new sex slang and television shows about digitally lined paper and television shows about the rich made for the rich they interpret poverty as such a glamorous party.

HISTORICAL SOCIETY

There is a great celebration. Researchers have just discovered that at some point in the 13th Century two years were misplaced on the Roman calendar. It was a confusing time. The Western World was ravaged by wars, disease, famine, and maybe Robin Hood if he was even real. It was nearly apocalyptic, and somewhere, somehow two years got skipped, and only now has a historical society realized the error of the past. It's agreed that the years will be turned back, and it's 2013 again. Everybody gets a second chance. A kid in Georgia reenrolls in school as an interpretive dance major rather than a biochemistry major. Two Minnesotan lovers reunite after an accusation-filled breakup and eat manicotti at their old favorite restaurant, although while they first dated, it was a Thai place. A cab driver returns all his Christmas gifts for store credit. He never liked them anyway. The government proclaims a week of celebration and feasting. Two years from now, everybody will be filled with great dread. They will have squandered everything, all their new chances. The checks will have been written, sent, and deposited. The lawyer who spent both new years stoned on his son's weed will check his stash box over and over again, but it will always be empty, a little ballerina spinning to a terminally slow *Swan Lake*. Everybody will claim disgust at even being given the two years to begin with. They will ask what difference a date's numbers mean, why the government even bothered to listen to the researchers. Still, every time they click on the news, they will hope the historical society will have found two more years. Or even just one. A day. Anything they can do over and make actually count this time.

SHOEBOX BOMB

Stiles and I wanted to make a bomb. We were thirteen, bored, girlfriendless. Kids at school had been making fun of me because I was Arab, saying I'd blow up the school. It was just after the World Trade Center bombing, the first "failed" one that only killed six people and that Biggie would immortalize in the lyric "blow up like the World Trade." Not that the kids at school needed a racial excuse to bully me—I had just moved from Canada and still called soda "pop," had tortoiseshell glasses, thick braces, and few friends other than Stiles, who was not exactly the Zack Morris of our middle school. I only mention the Arab thing though because Stiles figured I'd be a natural at building the bomb, it was in my blood. I only protested a little—my thirteen-year old self thought it would be pretty badass to have an innate bomb-making skill passed on through generations of badasses, for Arab terrorists, bad guys as they may be, were certainly badasses. The power to make something violent was seductive. So I grabbed a bunch of aerosol cans and batteries from my house, and we shoved it all into a shoebox with some M-80s. We took the box out to the woods and doused it in gasoline, then placed it on the bank of a stream and lit it on fire. It was a deep purple flame, and tall, maybe three or four feet. The batteries crackled in the flame and at every pop Stiles and I jumped back thrilled and terrified. A good ending to this story would be that the bomb exploded and we were injured, learning our lesson about becoming entwined in violence to cope with social inadequacies. What really happened was Miguel, another friend from the neighborhood, showed up and was scared, told us we'd get arrested if it exploded, so we pushed the bomb into the stream and doused it. It was foolish to cobble together all those explosives, but now as an adult I still regret that we didn't let it burn, let it detonate, that I didn't get as close as possible to the burst of flame to only barely avoid injury. I've blown up much bigger things since then, I've been seduced by fire and metal dozens of times. Miguel, it's like he fell off the planet, no social media, no nothing, and Stiles won't talk about the bomb, like it's some sexual experiment or torture we engaged in. Little failure crumpled in the woods. When my ass got kicked on the bus the next week and I bawled for the hour trip back from school, I just wanted to go home, I told my mother I wanted to leave my family behind and return to Canada, but Canada didn't exist anymore, nothing existed except the mottled roads of Lake City and its assemblage of endless fuses.

BORN AGAIN

The semester was long and brutal. A student, Geoff, didn't like the texts I assigned. He called them offensive to him as a Christian, and he wanted me to go through them to edit out all the blasphemy. I told him there was no way I could do that. "As a Christian," he said, "I can't read all these f-words." I felt bad for him, but he's an adult. More than an adult. A non-traditional student, as we call them. A 38 year-old sophomore creative writing major. "F-words were a part of my former life," he said. "I'm born again."

When I got this adjuncting position, the only training video they showed us was "Shots Fired on Campus: Dealing With A Live Shooter." You throw bookbags and chairs at them. You don't clump all your students together in a group, but spread out through the classroom so you're less easy to shoot. I don't mean to live in fear, but I always look at my students and wonder which one could do it, which one could be a live shooter.

The other students hand in stories with profanity. Geoff says in workshop to take it out, it'd be more serious if they said "Darn!" instead of "F!" and the readers could pay attention to the scene. We read professionally published stories with f-bombs in them, a poem about a blowjob. He says "It's *crap*," and emphasizes "crap" with such visceral emotion that the hipster next to him drops her phone. One student hands in a story about two abused daughters who shoot their father in the chest and escape. Geoff says that's too easy. "They should hit him in the face and blow off his jaw so it's hanging there. Then castrate him."

I dream I catch him at my house, pouring gasoline on

the lawn and front porch. I know he's spelling something. "What are you writing?" I ask. "You know what I'm writing," he says. "It's 'God,' isn't it?" I say. He nods and lights the gas on fire. "My wife's in there!" I say. "Well you better go save her," he says. He wrestles me to the ground and I can't move.

Geoff goes to the department head and complains about the university being anti-Christian because we read a story in which two men love each other, though that is not in and of itself the point of the story. The department head says Geoff held a cross necklace in his face, and sheepishly admits he told Geoff he'd have a word with me. "But they're *adults,*" I say.

Geoff always says he's a Christian like it's a rarity. Most of the people in that class are Christian, would call themselves Christian. He wears it like it's a contest. When I lost my virginity in high school, I walked around the next day at the mall looking at everyone, thinking that I had become a member of an elite club none of them would ever be a part of, but in reality most of those aimless teens in the food court probably lost their virginity long before I did, and more spectacularly then my two minutes of fumbling. Is it not enough to believe one is saved, one is loved by Jesus or God or whoever, that there is an unending escalator of pleasure and glory awaiting one in the afterlife? Why imagine one has to be alone to get the most grace? I didn't even want to lose my virginity but my girlfriend said I'd be a faggot if I didn't, that she'd tell everybody at school. That was years ago, we're still friends. The lights of the mall seemed brighter, but the night before I was in a bomb shelter in my girlfriend's arms. At the time, I never once imagined this might be grace.

HAMLET

Our baby was going to be born five months early. We thought it would die, but the doctors said they revolutionized a new medical technique, and they wanted us to try it out. The baby would have to live in a probiotic solution for the first two years of its life. It would be genderless, it would have no eyelids. "What about the cost?" we asked. "What about the human cost?" they replied. "Is it even a human yet?" we asked, but they had already drawn up the paperwork. We named the baby Hamnet. When family comes to visit, we take the baby carefully out of the probiotic solution, a mixture of yogurt and medicine in a small Tupperware container. They pretend to be happy, to be excited, but they are nervous. Hamnet has no eyelids, can only be viewed in dimmest candlelight. We lined our windows with tin foil like drug dealers. We take Hamnet out and say "Here is our pride and joy!" but nobody ever wants to hold the baby. We have to lower it into the probiotic solution gently, so we use a Kleenex that we pull apart at the last second, Hamnet falling the last centimeter into the yogurt, sinking in and wriggling a little bit. We want our baby to grow up and have a full life, a life full of loves and disasters, and the doctors are sure it will live. They have been right so far. "Is it of average intelligence?" we ask, nervously. The doctors say sure, but that instead of a brain there appears to be a writhing mass, a hive of bacteria and plankton. It could be the smartest creature on the planet, but we overheard our father say it was a bug with human meat. When we hold Hamnet in our palm, it darts its head around, it makes clicking noises with its tiny mouth. Too much air is a razor against its skin. Outside the city constantly rearranges itself, but when we emerge, the street names are back in their places, maybe only an inch or two off.

BODY IN THE DUMPSTER

I heard a voice while I was throwing out some pizza boxes from the kitchen into my apartment building's dumpster. It was faint, and I think it said "Help me." I looked around and couldn't see anybody. I walked behind the dumpster and there was nobody there. I said "Hello?" Again the voice, this time it definitely said "Help me." It came from inside the dumpster. I looked over the edge, but it was dark. I thought I could make out a hand, maybe. I said "Are you in there?" and the voice just said again "Help me." I started to lift myself over the edge, and a lot of flies were disturbed and flew up around me. There were also cockroaches, I'm sure. I couldn't quite make out movement in the trash. It smelled terrible, obviously, and I had to drop back down to the pavement to catch my breath. "Look," I said, "do you want me to come in after you? I could call for an ambulance." The voice again just said "Help me." I decided it was a joke. I wouldn't even call 911. Some kids probably laughing in one of the apartments around me. I almost fell for it, too, leaping into trash and bugs. So I just said "Fuck this." and left. I think the voice said "Help me" again. Back in my apartment, I washed the dumpster stink off my hands for ten minutes straight. If I had gone in I probably never could have gotten it off.

FALSE TEETH

Sarah loves Halloween. She puts weeks into preparing these parties, putting cobwebs on all our books, fake severed hands in each of our drawers. The parties are always hits. Everybody has Facebook photo albums of them from all different angles. This year Sarah went as a vampire. She got those fangs that they specially make, the really expensive ones, but she left them in even after the party, after Halloween. At first it was funny, like some kind of novelty. Everybody just saying "Oh, Sarah!" and getting back to work. But now it's almost December. Thanksgiving has passed. I said to her that it can't be good for her real teeth, to leave those fake ones in for most of the day. I wore mine just during the party, and my mouth hurt for two days. She said that was because I threw my werewolf costume together at the last minute and bought my fake teeth from a gas station. Hers were *real art*. I said it was probably time to take them out, people are talking. She just raised her arms above her head and said "Blood! I vant your blood!" It's tough to argue with her when she's being cute. I can't stand vampire movies, but when we started dating, I told Sarah I loved them. It's way past the point of no return on that lie. We actually have sex to the *Lost Boys* soundtrack a lot more frequently than I'd even care to admit. *People are strange, thou shalt not kill* spilling from the speakers. Jesus. Sarah's great, she's not like a goth or anything. But when does that road start? When we fight, she wishes aloud sometimes that "her romantic vampire" would just come and take her away. I don't know how I get jealous of that, but I do. Jealous of some imaginary creature that would never exist in a million years. And when we watch any new vampire movie, I just get furious secretly. The guys flash teeth, and I'm sure she's getting off on it. I can't picture my life after her, if she left, but I can feel the air being let out, the pressure letting up. I tell her she's pretty, she's the best, there's no end to my love. "Fangs a lot," she says.

DISFIGUREMENT

In orientation at my new job we go around to say where we went to college, and a bit about ourselves. Me, I went to Auburn, and I'm a Florida Panthers fan, *unfortunately*. Everybody laughs with politeness and ease. The guy at the end of my table stands up, and his face is twisted, malformed, like somebody tried to mold a face with clay that had gone too cold. He went to Georgia Tech and used to work in Central America as an engineer with a private security firm until a sniper shot him in the face from a long distance. We applaud him, but he seems ashamed of it, sits down quickly. I don't work in the same department as him or even on the same floor. He's in engineering and design, and I'm in advertising. Still, I keep bumping into him, a few times a day, and I try to smile and wave politely, but worry that he'll think I'm staring at his face. But what else am I supposed to look at? I'm trying to be polite without connection, wave or nod because we're *co-workers*, we must have the same general goals of success and upward mobility. My co-worker's face is mostly fine – he has two real, working eyes, a mouth, a nose-like hole where his nose should be. It's only mildly scary. Once on the train I sat across from a young woman. She was very pretty, too pretty to be on a train from New Orleans to Tallahassee. Our seats faced each other, and my eyes settled on her face even when I was trying to look at the blur of trees outside. At first she smiled, but it kept happening, my eyes kept landing on her face. She got angry, shifted in her seat and tried to look at her phone. I looked away but had to look back to see if she was still angry, and she looked back at me just as I looked back at her, and that happened four times before she told me to stop, she'd have me thrown off the train. I was sad that I upset her, I didn't mean to, but I was also angry that she saddened me by becoming upset. I got off at the next stop, Biloxi and let the train leave without me. It was morning in Biloxi, just before seven, and the streets were empty between the abandoned buildings. The train whistled away and I felt the wires pull free from my chest. Somebody had left a child's stuffed giraffe in front of the train station, next to a tall black ashtray that contained only dust and a dried piece of gum.

MACBETH

Macbeth stealing hubcaps and tossing them in the ditch. Macbeth pulling a wheelie on his BMX in heavy traffic, not giving a fuck. Macbeth yelling "Oops!" as he trips the nerdy kid. Lady Macbeth laughing, her hands around the neck of the truant officer. Macbeth skateboarding and not as a mode of transportation. Macbeth offering to shovel somebody's walk, then stealing their shovel when they tell him "No thanks." Macbeth at rest. Macbeth on edge, Robotripping. Macbeth imagining people who listen to him, who have to care. Lady Macbeth entering Macbeth's bedroom with peeled knuckles from a fistfight earlier. Macbeth rolling a sloppy joint. Macbeth running for class president because the guidance counselor thought being involved would at least help Macbeth get into community college. Macbeth victorious at the hands of an apathetic voting base. Macbeth pulling left, pulling right. Macbeth not replacing drinking fountains with soda fountains as promised. Lady Macbeth putting sugar in the vice principal's gas tank because she heard it'd make the car explode. Macbeth kicking a pony on a class trip. Macbeth on the bus. Macbeth with a seat to himself. Macbeth on a dirt road canopied by wild trees. Lady Macbeth putting out a cigarette on her own arm. Macbeth imagining a blade against his wrist. Macbeth eating a whole turkey avocado sandwich as a snack. Macbeth in an empty house, waiting for sound.

THE GROUP

We were meeting a group of friends for a Magic: The Gathering tournament in the Student Union building, but we had never been inside before, in all our time at the university. When we got to the front door there was a guy in a nice suit with a name badge: Dennis. We must have looked lost because he asked if we were with the group. We said yes, yes we were with the group. He told us up the stairs, lecture hall on the right. We did as he said, because it was true that we were with *a* group, and we were hoping the tournament would be large, as we had brought our rarest and most powerful cards. We got to the door of the lecture hall and another besuited guy asked if we were with the group. We told him, yes, we were with the group. We loved to be part of The Group. The Group was terrific. The Group was more powerful than he could possibly imagine. He opened the door and we found a seat near the back. Chairs were set up in rows facing a lectern – not ideal for a Magic tournament, not a sponsored one, anyway. We started to worry we weren't really part of The Group after all, but people filled in the chairs around us like sand pouring into a jar of marbles. Everybody was dressed up in suits and collared shirts, but we were wearing ripped jeans and shirts with funny 90s metal bands on them. Deicide, Biohazard, Cannibal Corpse. We still hoped whoever got up behind the lectern would talk about decks and tournament guidelines, but this was not our group though we had become inexorably entwined in it. A twenty-something dude with a fauxhawk in a long burgundy robe got up on stage, and everybody started cheering, some looking at the ceiling, some clutching their hands to their chests. When the guy started preaching some generic believe-in-yourself God stuff we were going to stumble out, but an image of a young woman that said 1992-2013 under it appeared behind him, and we thought it would be rude to leave. "She was driving home to see her sick grandmother," the dude said, "when she lost control of her car and it flipped on an icy back road." Murmurs rippled through the group. "When the paramedics got her body out of her car," he continued, "they said 'Spirit in The Sky'" was playing on loop through her stereo. A sign of Jesus!" Hands went in the air, people cheered and said "Amen!" and "Praise" and "Speak!" We wanted to make fun of it, the manipulation of death, but we were stuck, we were part of The Group now. Besides, a person really *did* die, or we presumed that the hip priest would not make *that* detail up. For all we knew she was formerly a part of The Group, all the members of The Group might know her and miss her dearly. This might be a memorial ceremony. Her image and the story of her death were part of The Group now at the very least, as were the murmurations, the fauxhawk, us and our desire to play Magic: The Gathering with friends. As a child I walked into my parents' room at dawn, the sun low in the sky. My father was still asleep but I wanted to talk to him, I had a dream he let an orb of light in through the front door. When I entered their room, the sun shone through the window in a way to place the shadows of icicles on the wall near the ceiling. I screamed—it was as though the outside world had invaded the home—icicles were hanging from my parents ceiling even though I knew they were really outside. Once the idea of icicles in the room existed, so existed icicles in the room, inseparable from truth. In the lecture hall, the girl next to us is crying and burying her face in her friend's chest. A recording of a gospel choir spills from the hall's mediocre sound system and everybody starts swaying.

CLOWN,
WITH MAGGOTS IN MOUTH

At my college boyfriend's undergraduate art show, there was a piece called "Capitalism," a life-size sculpture of a clown head with tiny detailed maggots flowing from its mouth. I looked away from it, was repulsed, and instinctively grabbed my boyfriend's arm. He laughed at my reaction, and I said the art was bad, was trite and purposely ridiculous. He said that's the point, the artist is saying capitalism is also bad, gross, oppressively trite. I said big fucking deal, and he got angry at me, saying I just didn't understand art. It bothered me to be bothered by such a stupid sculpture, to have my revulsion laughed at. Yeah, I agree capitalism sucks, but I didn't ask to look at a grotesque clown on a Wednesday evening. Did the piece make me feel differently about the world? Grossed out about clowns a bit and of course I continued my lifelong distaste for maggots, but show me someone who actually likes maggots, even the medical kind, which I must add are only typically used as a last resort on gangrenous wounds. At night, I couldn't sleep, I kept thinking about that fucking clown, so I spent hours googling car accident death photos, people crushed by tractor trailers on freeways, one person eviscerated in a smart car accident. It didn't bother me. None of it bothered me as much as the clown. I dug deep through the rotten.com archives, looked at videos of people shooting themselves, jumping off high buildings, but it just made me angrier and angrier at the clown sculpture. I wanted to buy stocks. I wanted to ditch my Socialist Party card. I called my boyfriend the next morning and said it just wasn't working out. He said he didn't want to be with a philistine anyway, and that also I was kind of a bitch lately, and that also he had cheated on me with one of his professor's graduate assistants. This was years ago. If I'm alone in my home and I need to wake up early, my brain still pulls up that clown, maggots pouring out of its mouth, and I'm up for hours more. My ex became a corporate lawyer, and a mutual friend says he pulls in a half a million dollars a year but he's "not happy." Me, I'm trying to get my plays produced by the community theater and am on food stamps. I'm also "not happy." Are we both victims? What ridiculous wounds have we been letting fester all this time?

THE COLOR BEARERS
OF THE SPRING BRIGADE

In elementary school there was a proto-ROTC military group for grades three through five called the Spring Brigade. Kids would join, pay some money for a fake military dress uniform, and learn to march in parades and go camping. I hated the outdoors but my best friend, Isaac, joined, and so I figured I had to join too. I wasn't exactly part of the cool crowd in rural Maine. I had big thick glasses and loved science fiction. In everyday school situations I'd wear Spider-Man sweatshirts and sweatpants that matched. In a town of almost all white families I was one of the darkest kids, Arab, though at the time I didn't know what to call myself. A couple kids called me the n-word at recess on a regular basis and pushed me around. I thought the word just meant "booger," but I still didn't like it. I joined the Spring Brigade, and Isaac and everyone got to carry cool wooden rifles during the parade. They ran out just before they got to me, although I was not last alphabetically, and said I could have the most important job of all, the color-bearer. I'd get to carry the flag of the United States of America and march at the front of the pack, and while it did sound like it bore some responsibility, I would rather run around the church basement with a wooden rifle like everybody else. On our first practice run in the church parking lot, I was told to rest the flag against my right shoulder while marching. It was much heavier than I thought, and as soon as we were called to attention, I fumbled and dropped the flag on the ground, it slowly teetering forward like a drawbridge being lowered. Our leader, who asked that we call him Corporal Buddy, ran over yelling for us not to touch it. It was disappointing, he said, looking at me, that the flag was not held above the ground honorably, but now it had to be respectfully disposed of by fire. He separated the flag from its pole and bunched it into the middle of the parking lot. He lit it after a few tries with his Zippo lighter. Everybody in the Spring Brigade stared at the burning fabric with awe, and I felt power, I felt I didn't need a wooden rifle, that I brought the flag to flames and everyone respected me because of this moment. I had to practice with an empty pole for a while until Corporal Buddy could get approval from the Spring Brigade home office to buy a new flag from our rainy day cash. The new flag came just in time for the high school homecoming parade. I was good at marching, at maintaining the proper stance for holding a flag, but I wanted to get that respect of a kid who could compel an adult to start a fire at a moment's notice. At the end of the parade, during which middle school kids threw poppers at our feet, I purposely fumbled a shoulder switch and let the flag fall to the ground. It hit bottom of the pole first, and Corporal Buddy yelled for me to catch it, but I overacted in my wild swing and miss. The jig was up. The Corporal screamed at me in front of everybody for disrespecting our country, our country's flag, everybody who had ever died for all our freedoms and to stop us from speaking Chinese. I cried because I couldn't handle an adult screaming at me like that. Isaac asked if we would burn the flag, and Corporal Buddy said yes, but that I wouldn't be allowed to attend. Later that week, we had a meeting with the Corporal and my mother. Corporal Buddy told my mother I wasn't Spring Brigade material and my time would probably be spent better elsewhere, maybe with other immigrant children. My mother said I wasn't an immigrant and asked if I could just be allowed to carry the state flag, because nobody really cared about Maine, and I could drop the flag all day without repercussions. Corporal Buddy said no, it was over, and that also we could not get our deposit for the year back. I was sad because my mother was disappointed, but the flag is just a flag. Yes, I wanted it burned, I wanted that power, but I was nine years old, and who, even as an adult, can't say they've been seduced by the power of fire? And Buddy was wrong anyway, there's no law that says you've got to burn a flag that touches the ground. Isaac and me stayed friends, and he hated camping, ended up getting bitten up by leaches. The ringleader of the kids who called me the n-word later wound up hanging himself in the woods in high school, and I felt sorry for him. Corporal Buddy got accused of falsifying his own military service, but then he drowned saving a family on a sinking boat in the Bay of Fundy. I'll never regret making those flags get burned, but I know I still let him down, I let them all down, somehow, and it stuck webbed in a corner of their skulls until they died.

THE WOODEN PUPPY

When I was a kid I had a wooden puppy I loved. I could pull it around on a string, and its wheels would make a kind of croaking noise, more like a frog though I knew it was supposed to be a doggish growl. We moved around a lot, so I didn't really make friends that stuck. Instead I had a lot of favorite toys, toys I loved. A robot who could change, if you knew the precise sequence of twists, into a handgun. A giant, plastic stealth bomber filled with little replicas of warplanes used throughout the decades. I loved the puppy but could not play with the puppy in front of friends, or even alone, in case a friend came into the room without announcement or pomp. I moved away to college after high school— rather, my parents moved two weeks after I finished high school and let me stay to go to college. On my own, I had the freedom to stay up until four a.m. watching infomercials and to eat burgers six times a week. One day before class I heard a mewling, a little squeak from outside, and found, nudged up against the outside wall of my apartment, four kittens in a puddle of rainwater. Only one was still alive and only barely. I took it to the vet and said "It'll make it, right?" and the vet lauded my efforts, though, of course, the last kitten didn't make it. I finished college and got a cat, two cats, little biological toys I could pull from apartment to apartment. Now I'm married and my wife loves the cats, speaks to them as if they're her kids. I can't help but wonder if that wooden puppy got abandoned in some move. Can we only pump the tires of love once and coast until death? My wife, my cats, our meager home and income—a system of energy and light I wish I could seal off forever from the elements.

WITNESS PROTECTION

My neighbor didn't have many friends. I rarely saw him go out. Whenever I saw him in the halls of the fourplex we lived in, he seemed jumpy. Just a quick nod. He was always carrying Burger King bags. He wasn't out of shape, but he wasn't a "paragon of good health." I would go weeks without seeing him, then suddenly him, the bags, the nod. This time wasn't any different from those other lonely weeks, except there was the smell. Like sour almonds and meat. It got so that it was tough to walk by his door. I had already guessed what had happened before I called the landlord. His body was found lodged against the door and had been dead for at least fifteen days. A real mess, maintenance said. Nobody knew if he had family or not. His tennis buddy came by and was shocked. The tennis buddy said he didn't have a phone, would schedule all their matches by pay phone. He was sad to miss the service, but I didn't know if there even was a service. Two guys in suits came by. They said he had been in witness protection, asked if there was anything strange I wanted to tell them about. I said nothing, just that smell. So bad I had to sleep on a friend's couch for a week. They didn't leave a card. What I said wasn't totally true, though. Before my neighbor had died, or maybe right around when he died, I heard a sound. A groan from behind the walls. I thought he was masturbating. Maybe crying. I didn't want to get involved. But what if he had been choking? Having a heart attack? If I had tried to help, maybe he'd be alive. Maybe I would be able to knock on his door and do a good thing, a neighborly thing. Lend him an egg. Play chess. What neighbors do. The people downstairs in the fourplex moved out. They were an intelligent modern couple but worried about his ghost, stranded by all his loneliness, all his misery. What justice is there in this world to lead us to think that even in death we can't escape our hurt. Our suffering extends beyond our flesh. Here in this neighborhood is a free museum filled with hundreds of paintings depicting all the varieties of sorrow. The museum is lit naturally, with screens and reflectors diffusing sunlight down and into every corner, drowning the little shadows out. What a generous gift that heiress left us oh those many years ago.

COLLAPSIBILITY

1. PENDULUM WITH BLADE TIED TO THE BOTTOM

Is this the relief an American home was to offer? The solid ground beneath your feet. The sky creeping into your breath. The news anchors put you to sleep. The interstate exit churns dread. No more, no more. The plaque reads "We came in peace for all mankind." Cry wolf. Cry predator. No one will believe you anyway.

2. THE RISING POPULATION

Love, that bane of heart, creeps in under the skin. Throats are torn open. Words are spilled to the floor. The busload of immigrants always dreamed of coming to America, of beginning again here in The City. They, too, break like balsawood under stone.

3. PEOPLE WHO ARE STRANGERS TO US

Our fears swim the air around us like clothesline sheets. In every driveway, cars start to rust into skeletal hulks. If we dared to walk outside, we would instantly be embraced by one of our endlessly sobbing neighbors. But in this world, we have done no good.

4. VANDALS DEFACING GRAVESTONES

Our skin could fetch our necks a rope. Our hearts could draw us a bloody wire. What was love now curdles to hurt. Who can live well and know that man is so vile to hate man to death? The city has announced the parks will be slowly ravaged by jackhammers. Then the playgrounds. The fair-haired traffic cop ripped up our ticket. Our fatal flaw is our capacity for forgiveness, she said.

5.   ABSOLUTION

Try not to be sorry her mantel photograph doesn't mean anything anymore. We can't be responsible for all the words we've said. Old poisons. Old flasks and rusting weapons. There is always something formal about a gun's muzzle.

6.   ONE FULL YEAR

Finally, the words have become official—winter, night, the cycling deaths of trees and gravestones moved out of the city. No one can know the depth of rot, unless it is in the ropes of hanging ballasts snapped over actors in classic tragedies, their injuries mourned by all who attend.

7.   A PUBLIC DISPLAY

The reservoir that runs through the city has drowned a dozen lovesick souls this year alone. It runs right through the downtown corridor. In our custom, unwanted dogs are sealed in barrels of rocks and pushed into the lakes. Who can leave such strings untied? Later, we are doomed to finish our struggle.

8. YOU CAN NEVER BE ALONE HERE

On the table, a bedside drink. Ambulance lights flash through the blinds. Another neighbor. First, there was hope, before words slithered from throats. Before a rock was struck against another for the sake of rhythm. What was second? Now we're at the bottom, with the rocks and current. Do we welcome the water or writhe in defeat?

AUDIO CASSETTE BOUGHT FROM GOODWILL MARKED "KELLY"

At first, static. Almost two minutes. Then, a cough. Gentle, as if calmly getting someone's attention. A moan—a woman—and springs. The slide of a metal chain across the floor. A man's fast breath. Woman begging *please...oh, please.* Some wet skin and awkward rhythm. A pause. Something wooden is dropped. Then the rustle of papers, like applause.

STITCHES

When there was some place to go at five when the time clock automatically punched me out, then I sped out, my plum Pontiac taking me coolly down the streets of Tallahassee and to the bar with fake rain sprayed onto the outside of the windows to meet up with a friend or two, or to a second-run movie on fifty-cent Tuesday. There wasn't usually someplace to go. My friend who got me the temp job at Stitches, the T-shirt factory, was a full-timer, she had to stay, to load boxes if there was a rush order, the bosses chanting the mantra of unity. I'd wait in my car, we'd drive back into town and sometimes sleep together if time and body pushed us to it. Me, I believed in unity. This was the third job I had in a row that made me sign an agreement that unions are the undoing of America. I needed money. Tallahassee is only a place you can stand with a couple bucks and a couple beers. We made T-shirts for Coke, for Walk America. I was not usually on the floor, I was carrying documents and orders from office to foremen. Loading boxes when Atlanta called, the bigger orders. A factory for Coke shirts, it sounds like a joke, a factory that makes the screens of fruit for slot machines. To worship a corporation is to worship a megalith of metals, plastics, warships and bone. Now, years later, the news chides the protests, says they are aimless, runs a sad story when the CEO dies, his products and profit brought us so much joy. Midway knighted itself The T-Shirt Capital of Florida to honor the factory, the jobs. All companies are glorious, slinking across the land with wings dragging behind them, throwing immense shadows down upon towns. Those who are in drought hope it means rain, and those scorched are thankful for the shade. I loved my friend years before, my coworker, but even by the time we worked together it was only the mist of memory conjured by the scents of some florid industrial soaps or a painful smile in the right dim light.

INTERFERENCE

The other day I was running at a track that loops around the private university in town. This woman in front of me was running while pushing her baby in one of those running strollers. Her baby threw its pacifier out of the stroller, and it landed on the ground in front of me. I almost picked it up, but I would've had to stop, and I was at my optimal heart rate. Plus, what if she got crazy about some stranger germing up her kid's pacifier. I ran by, actionless. I have been getting stronger and faster. When running I try to keep my breathing steady because somebody once told me we each have a certain number of breaths allotted to us from birth. Sure, it's dumb, but we can't help the traps we fall into. I run four times a week. On one side of the university there are lush trees and rows of McMansions. On the other side they are building many towering hospitals. Giant cranes frame the sky. A worker fell to his death from one on a day I don't run. Each crane hovers over the skeletal beginnings of hospitals designed by architects to look organic and welcoming. When I see a pigeon dart out in front of me while I run I am still astonished by the beautiful and intricate patterns on its back, and these are just the birds we all call sky rats.

GOLD HALOS

My husband is a ridiculous animal lover. He has two cats, and the only reason he doesn't have more is because when we were dating, before we were married, I hesitated when he asked if I'd dump him if he got a couple more cats. Maybe I wouldn't have really dumped him, but it's already a constant battle not to have the smell of cat piss waft over everything we own. About a month ago, we saw a dog get hit by a car, on Tennessee St., and it pushed my husband over I think. The dog just darted out of a bar, Tinsels, and into the street. Two cars missed it, but it went right under a pickup truck. He cried right there on the street, in front of drunk strangers and undergrads. I love animals, yes, but now my husband stops the car when we see roadkill, places a gold binder ring on the dead animal's head like a halo. When I'm on a long bike ride, I sometimes don't even swerve away from smaller roadkill if my speed is up, if the roadkill is flat. It's not much different than riding over a pile of leaves, although more than once my front tire has kicked up a bone that has bounced off my bare leg, which is pretty gross. I love my husband's sensitivity, his web to all creatures, but it's childish, these halos, it's filling our lives with inconvenience. Most of these creatures would attack my husband if they met him in life, if they were cornered. Me, I've made him cry and meant to, then soothed him afterward, holding him in my arms tight and whispering into his ear. That's what being in love is about—knowing when to levy the lash in order to sweeten the embrace.

CHOOSE
YOUR OWN ADVENTURE

Your father has been killed in a hit-and-run accident. If you wish to:

- Make a record of things destroyed on film, turn to page 38.
- Realize it's never too early to start writing songs about your own death, turn to page 89.
- Gaze deeply into the speculum of fire, turn to page 17.
- Get out your old bottles of glitter and glue, turn to page 28.
- Slowly count the nation's newsworthy dead, turn to page 63.
- Call your ex-boyfriend who calls himself a poet, turn to page 89.
- Look for the hidden door, turn to page 3.
- Use Google to find out what the hell a speculum of fire is, turn to page 92.
- Prove the old masters knew dick about love, turn to page 101.
- Wear your old jacket against the cold, turn to page 32.
- Check the abandoned and rotting house deep in the woods without bringing a candle or friend for comfort, turn to page 9.
- Get lost in photographs and cry over the futility of it all, turn to page 12.
- Bake a big chocolate cake and eat the whole thing by yourself, turn to page 13.
- Write a poem about the uniqueness of your suffering, turn to page 1.
- See a sad movie about dystopia and eat a big bag of buttered popcorn and peanut M&Ms during it, turn to page 81.
- Grieve, turn to page 327.

- Build a fort out of blankets and the couch and live there for a few days, turn to page 74.

- Move to California and do a lot of acid, turn to page 19.

- Win a hot air balloon racing contest and then give the award money to charity, turn to page 24.

- Call the police commissioner who considers himself a poet and turn in the real killer, turn to page 50.

- Gaze deeply at the words "speculum of fire," turn to page 79.

- Come to terms with something terrible and then convince your friends to do the same, turn to page 6.

- Forever give up on the worth of a gym membership, turn to page 67.

- Consider yourself one of the lucky few who still live, turn to page 59.

- Sweep up the broken light bulb from the kitchen floor, turn to page 41.

OTHER MARKS
MADE BY CURRENTS

On the table is an academic catalog of literature written from the perspective of the dead, the happy dead ensconced in heavens of nostalgia, regret tingeing their voices, long ago, things happy and never happy again, the confused dead, the dead who do not realize they are dead, the wrongfully dead and the justly dead, the dead in whose death the reader played a hand though they wish to pretend their politics absolve them from responsibility, the dead rock stars, actors, politicians, all immortalized in T-shirts but speaking again on the page, the dead we are happy to see dead, the dead who get their revenge by adding the living to their numbers, the dead who knock over glass elephants on the counter to get the attention of their still-living lovers, the dead who manifest only as thoughts or voices from around a corner in dreams, a spot on a window, the dead who may be approaching us in a crowd, the dead who live just beyond the line of trees we never dare to enter. And me, waiting here, listening to an old country and western recording, the accidental scrape of a guitar pick against the string, the brief smack of the singer's lips as he is about to take a breath.

BABY MODEL

When I was a baby, an infant, maybe under six months old, my father brought me to an agent who specialized in young models. I had headshots taken, smiling and leaning on a toy block of the letter "B." I modeled until I was six, when I was in a "Fashion of Spain" show and didn't walk in a straight line. There were adults saying my posture was terrible. The gown was colorful, like a package of birthday napkins. I would have to miss school for gigs or leave from school to go to interviews. We had a black nylon bag with a yellow hairbrush and books for entertainment. My father had acting experience, I saw him in an off-off Broadway play where he played a doctor. No. He just saw the modeling as a way to have savings for college. He and my mother didn't make much money. I was a happy baby, and ads needed happy babies. When I was two or three, on an interview, I walked around the waiting room kissing all the younger babies on the head until one mother got mad. She said "Stop, you'll mess up her hair." Being happy is important to me, thank you. I didn't want to sit still and smile. There was a lot of waiting around without a guarantee and no satisfaction if I did get the job. It's not like I was running out to buy the Ambesol box and saying "That's me!" I enjoyed acting more, but you must devote your whole life to it if you want to succeed. It's a waste of the limited hours we have. I do like to move around. I like to go on walks, I like to dance. Hip hop, oldies, Motown, Top 40 girl pop singers. Rock music is for dumb sluts. I understand that what we choose to put forward in the social world in terms of face, words, and posture can affect a certain judgment. You can control how others see you. If you want to elicit a state of emotions or responses, control is important. I feel bad for the child models now because they can't pack up the black nylon bag and go home. Their parents probably have huge empty lives, fantasize about beauty and acclaim. They themselves never realize it. I don't think it matters. The model in the ad is not the point. It's only The Product. The child is never acknowledged. They don't have to be haunted by it.

WADING

The new boy was beautiful, and I wanted him to be my friend, and only mine. Our teacher introduced him to the class. He moved here from Atlanta. We were rural Florida, real Spanish moss trailers and Food Lion grocery trips. The new boy, Cyril, had blue eyes that glittered like television static. He was tall for a ninth grader, maybe pushing six feet. I said I'd show him around campus. In my mind I knew I wasn't a faggot. Outside homeroom I took him by the hand, I took his hand in mine and not in the fashion of a leader. I jerked off to the idea of girls, yes, but Cyril and his eyes were churning up my lungs. I could picture us entwined in each other's limbs, wrestling, at first, then breathing together, then the hard bones of our skulls kissing. Cyril didn't let go of my hand, he just said "careful." There was a kid in middle school band, Marcus, that everybody knew was gay. Me and two friends got assigned to a room with him on a trip, and my friends told me to tell the band director, Mr. Hofner, to change our room. I didn't want to, knew it was mean but also didn't want to seem "OK with Marcus." I told Mr. Hofner we needed a new room, without Marcus, and he asked me why. I said because Marcus is not straight. Mr. Hofner was my favorite teacher, but he yelled at me, told me to get real, to grow up, and I knew he lost respect for me. We roomed with Marcus, and he turned out to be a cool guy, we all liked him, though my friend Aaron would not split the bed with him and slept on the floor. The codes of overnight trips with other boys: never lay facing each other, never tell each other "good night." Don't get me wrong—we did not become friends with Marcus after the trip, and Marcus did not want to be friends with us. At the beginning of ninth grade, a group of baseball players kicked Marcus's ass in the cafeteria, called him gay boy, busted his front teeth out, and we all joined in yelling "fight, fight, fight," though it was not a fight. I only had a few friends, see, with whom I did not speak of anything besides our shared miseries—rural loneliness and the isolation of our bus rides home into the black north Florida woods.

CARNIVALIA

The calendar. The omega. The glory. The glass. The content. The story. The filth. The mouse. The answer. The marathon. The monitor. The wires. The envelope. The absence. The dancer. The liar. The happens. The art. The brush. The careening. The rush. The murder. The save. The elephantitis. The pillowcase. The roadblock. The rock. The grass. The yellow. The constellation. The star. The view. The far. The window. The allegory. The content. The story. The form. The dismantle. The hollowing. The box seats. The goal. The dime. The management. The contact information. The call. The holler. The cat. The rib. The Hamlet. The rub. The eye. The nerve. The I get it. The speed dial. The catch. The hundred and ten. The back. The rub. The release. The beast. The understood. The tense. The bloodstain. The common product. The alpha. The fifty stars. The road trip. The content. The forty. The sleepwalking. The waking. The on the road by. The clock. The cock. The skirt. The issue. The release. The center line. The seat tray. The flagellation. The semicolon. The bread. The basket. The mouse. The answer. The never asked. The still. The stamp. The college. The collage. The interpretive. The desire. The line. The release. The close. The cleanliness. The blind. The window. The allegory. The doctor's orders. The order. The ejection. The ruin. The perforate. The misperception. The wrung. The second floor. The stairwell. The ink. The coal. The showerhead. The drink. The music collection. The star. The true. The far. The recyclable. The dime. The lens. The emergency break. The holler. The call. The book binding. The follow. The river. The drowning. The caffeine. The compact disc. The juggernaut. The myth. The Harlem. The bitch. The origination. The state. The of. The unity.

The "Wanna Be Startin' Somethin'." The hall. The river. The dance. The beat. The open wound. The stitch. The frowned upon. The clitoris. The release. The water. The quick. The holistically. The stick. The education. The camera. The evidence. The rib. The sensationally. The trip back home. The cityscape. The magazine. The roil. The postcard. The filled out already. The content. The effervescent. The royal. The broken. The story. The mean. The desire. The peg. The release. The protocol. The standard. The the. The acquiesce. The hold me. The rudimentary. The statutory. The content. The riverbed. The story. The collections. The holding company. The doctor's. The orders. The chain. The link. The ocean or drink. The ash. The air. The belonging. The hung. The where. The plank. The hovering spirit. The brink. The '76. The confusion. The holy holy. The card. The cards. The it's not in it. The saintly. The something. The I'm. The give me now. The champion. The glory. The cause. The sorry. The accidental. The inflections. The dog. The dead. The other rib. The tool. The breast. The shirt. The collapse. The release. The stranded in fleece. The hunch. The escape. The trapped by concrete. The sun. The ray and the cancer. The bully. The dancer. The runaround. The Sue. The follow up. The rinse. The ability to forgive. The take and keep taking.

WATER IN ITS THREE FORMS

I.

In March, in fifty-degree weather, my friend convinces me to walk out across a frozen pond. He slams a log into it to show me it's safe. He wants my help grabbing an old hockey puck. I walk across the pond, despite all the school videos showing us not to, and we both fall through. The water is only up to our chests. My friend's mother screams at us for an hour when we get home, but I don't get in trouble with my own parents. Two weeks later a girl from the grade below us drowns after falling through a different pond. My mother cries in her room with the door closed. That night, an animal leaves an eviscerated duck beside our porch.

II.

In college, three of us drive across the state to the beach, even paying a sudden thirty dollar toll, because my friend Ana has a crush on our friend Jeff who is at home for the summer. We go swimming even though the red flags are up. The waves are incredible, higher than a human. If we aren't careful, it is like bellyflopping sideways each time they hit. Our friend Kim's top keeps getting knocked off by the waves, but Ty, who years later we learn is gay, is the only one who ever sees it happen. That night we head back to Jeff's house, and he and Ana have a long talk in his room while the rest of us hang out on the back porch. A palmetto bug crawls across my hand and I try to be cool about it, but I end up crying a bit. Ty and Kim say it's ok, it's just a bug, but this only makes me cry more. I am older than them and graduating, and I know this is the last time we'll all hang out together.

III.

My babysitter when I am seven likes to make tea. I am obsessed with the scream of the kettle, the quickness of the manufactured cloud. Once, twenty minutes after her tea is done, I am patting my hands across the counter and stove. I did not realize the burner would still be hot, and I gasp suddenly in pain. The fear in my babysitter's eyes makes me want to amplify my hurt, to wallow in a place where I, briefly, am more powerful than she is. She says she's sorry, she's sorry, she shouldn't have made tea in the first place.

THE VOICES

Dark grey clouds are pressed together over us, and streaks like red veins run between them, the whole terrible blanket pulled from east to west, the sun hidden, and all the ground dark with its color pulled out. The news tells us it is wildfires hundreds of miles away, that ash and flame have crept on wind to our small town, and all the towns around us, and all the towns between us and the fire, and towns even further away from the burning forest than us, and we're all witnesses to the traveled flame. Here an old woman has crawled in her nightgown into the street, and we watch her slap the pavement until her hands are black and bleeding, and she screams to the Lord above to spare us his wrath and writhes on her back and tells the sky she has been a good woman, that her neighbors are good people, that we don't deserve his flaming sword drawn across our backs or a bloody shower from the sky, and we know her husband has been dead only four months, and we should let her seep this out alone in the road, not with audience, but most of us are on our porches to begin with, to stare at the sky. She says "Oh Lord, forgive us." She says "Oh Lord, it's the end." We know it's the end. The other day while helping a friend move, he lifted an old box of books from his shed and a hundred cockroaches crawled out and onto his arm, a twisting gauntlet of moving black oil sheen, and a bright, white eye appeared in the moving mess, a bright orb on a black wolf, and when finally we got them all off and my friend calmed down, there were bite marks, hundreds of small, red dots, constellations on his arm, a few on his face and neck, and his girlfriend ran into the house and locked herself in their bedroom. In the pile of dead roaches, the ones we managed to kill, there was a white roach, an albino. Before, in dreams, I have painted walls only to have them start moving, then the painted roaches crawl off of the walls, pushing up through the paint like newborns, and stumbling after me for revenge. Now the dreams are becoming realized. This could be one of the legendary plagues. The woman in the street is done. She is escorted back to her porch. It starts to rain. It's thick and black and stings our eyes. It poisons our gardens. It stains our windows. It destroys our reservoirs. The children run from the swings to the roofed-in porch. The roads become slick as though with black ice, and cars slide into lampposts and ditches and off the edges of the highest bridges. For weeks, there have been voices heard in the cemetery. Though nobody can make out what the voices in the cemetery are saying, everybody who has heard them agrees the voices are nervous. Above us, the seams crack open.

COLLUSION

Evan and I stopped by unannounced to Murray's house to hang out. We were in seventh grade, and Murray's dad was never around, which made his house great to hang out and at least pretend we were schemers or smokers or something cooler than a bunch of nerds trading superhero cards. Murray was happy to see us, but he warned us that Kevin had basically invited himself over and that basically he'd be there any minute. Kevin was our friend, or, at least, he was with us at the bottom of the social pool, and so we hung out with him, but he was always so full of energy, and we just wanted to sit around and watch TV. Kevin would want to light fires or talk about masturbation or walk downtown to buy cheap gummy candy. We decided that Evan and I would hide upstairs, amidst the junk in the attic, and Murray would tell Kevin his dad was coming home early and he'd get in trouble if he had guests. Evan and I hid up in the attic, just under the lone circular window above the back porch where Kevin would arrive. The house was the oldest house any of us knew, with an unfinished basement with a dirt floor we'd imagine corpses buried underneath. We hoped for ghosts, or talked excitedly about ghosts, but there was never anything there, no proof of an afterlife for us preteen dorks. Kevin showed up after about ten minutes of Evan and me stifling giggles in the attic. We heard Murray tell Kevin the father story, but Kevin was unsure, was paranoid Murray was just trying to ditch him. Kevin started to buy it eventually, and I was proud of our ruse, of our collusion. I felt like the lie was worthless without being discovered. I danced a desk lamp with a long neck past the window, and Evan and I started laughing. Kevin figured us out, and we had to hang out with him, we couldn't just say we wanted him gone. I said I wanted Kevin to think the place was haunted, that the lamp flew past the window on its own, but Kevin said he knew it was us, he knew it was us all along.

DEGREES

It was summer and I needed to find a job, stat. I had just gotten my MFA in studio art, but it turns out art is for suckers. I called my parents to ask for advice and my father said hit the pavement. That's the same thing he said when I finished high school ten years ago, but, well, maybe good advice doesn't evolve. The summer was nothing but record highs. My A/C broke and the landlord said there was absolutely nothing he could do about it. I checked with the museum, but they needed experience and a business degree. The local oil companies were hiring like crazy, but you needed a Bachelor's of Oil Studies. I like cop shows, so I called the police department, but I'd never even held a gun. The local schools wouldn't return my calls, and even the movie theater sent me a rejection card in the mail. The elderly regularly died of heatstroke, but that was normal. A kid though had to be airlifted out of a park for burning the backs of her legs on a metal slide. On the news they said to stay indoors at all costs. Nobody could be held accountable they said. In this city the anxiety of millions of people increased and the heat rose. Even the pool was too hot. Somebody said that art no longer fit into society and I couldn't argue with them. Bottled water was selling at all-time highs. People drove their cars relentlessly.

TALLEST PERSON/ SHORTEST PERSON

In our town lives the tallest person in the world, at 8'11". I am 5'10", not tall exactly, and when I am walking on various errands around town or for leisure I sometimes see this tallest person, a man with a beard who always wears a suit, and I will wave to him, yet he does not always wave back, though I do not think this is because of any sort of unfriendliness but rather that he may not see me, being that I am, despite being a full-grown average adult male, almost half his height. "Hello, tallest person!" I imagine saying to him. "We live in different worlds!" I wonder if he possesses the same sort of brain that I do, since it is twice the size of my brain, or if he has twice the number of thoughts I do, twice the nuisances, twice the miseries. I think of children, their chatter and running about, how they have their own languages and phrases that I never understand. The tallest person works at a law firm in town as a paralegal. You may expect that he played basketball at some point, but no, as I read him saying in an interview, his extreme size puts such a pressure on his bones that—even to walk—he must wear a brace. The shortest person in the world is a woman in Mexico who is just around a foot and a half tall. She is a college student and has made the honor roll according to an Internet site I read. If the shortest person in the world, the college student in Mexico, and the tallest person in the world, the aloof paralegal here, met, they would be like aliens to each other, and she could perch on his shoulder and give him angelic and/or devilish advice, though the same sort of thoughts would run through both of their heads as run through my head, questions about adequacy or inadequacy, a fear of being stepped on or stepping on another, the general sort of navigation around hurt in which we are all engaged. If the shortest person in the world would be like an alien to me, I am not sure—the tallest person in the world is in a different world, and my average neighbor is in a different world because she is a doctor, and my mother is in a different world because she does not know how to use her cell phone to respond to text messages. "Hello, doctor!" I imagine saying to my neighbor. "Hello, mother!"

THE CAPE BRETON SCREAMING EAGLES

When White Juan came in, the blizzard of 2005, they had to cancel home games for the local junior hockey club for two weeks. Steven, who had grown up in Sydney and moved back there after med school, was shell-shocked. The Eagles were his passion. He loved everything having to do with his home, and to see them defeat anybody, especially the Halifax Mooseheads, was one of his few moments of exhilaration. He was very busy and successful. He had a wonderful Lebanese-Canadian wife. He loved his hometown. The landscape of it all, the cliffs a short drive away, the beaches. Nova Scotia is a land of great beauty say a lot of people, but Steven thought that beauty was mostly concentrated in Cape Breton. There's nothing wrong with loving the place you're from, but a lot of people probably think Steven is being ridiculous. Some people move around their whole lives and never feel any tug from the ground that isn't gravity. Not many people trust geography. I was going to say that Steven's father died in the blizzard, but we're all assaulted by grief eventually. I sometimes think there is just too much for me to handle in this world, Lord, oh Lord.

CELESTE CELESTE

Was the pilot's call sign. Was the name of his girlfriend back in Tallahassee. Was the queen of her prom. Wore a dress that looked like a cake. Was the end of an era of unfucked nights. Was an aspiring novelist. Was obsessed with change on a personal level. Was a former meat eater. Was enamored with anything rust-colored. Was a hunter of used LPs. Was a college radio DJ. Was the photo on the mirror surrounded by smudged glue. Was a real girl, a real American girl. Was guarded. Shot guns. Believed in the working class. Was a supporter of the troops. Bring them home. Was the kind of thing you could get stuck in. Was a real dream, a real American dream. Voted third party in every election. Sunk ships. Was the pilot's girlfriend back in Tallahassee. Was a made-up name to begin with. Believed in Jesus and in true sin. Didn't know how or even where to begin.

KISSIMMEE MIDDLE SCHOOL

I am in an Italian restaurant, perhaps the only one in Osceola County, I am an alien here, a stumbling cloud. I am suffering through seventh grade again, this time as the teacher. My students yell at me, one throws a chair across the room. This makes them sound like the villains, but I am a bad teacher, just out of college with no classroom experience. The other teachers tell me to just get in the kids' faces and scream wildly to control them. In this restaurant, I am meeting a coworker who makes me uncomfortable. She has told me the sexual things she would do to me if she was younger, running her hands through my hair, the blowjobs she would give, were she her younger self. She has told me of the handguns she owns. I have a hard time telling people no when they wear hurt slung over their shoulders. This woman, I do not like her. She seems violent, she scares me. I can not extricate myself from her. She invites me over to watch *Gone with the Wind*, her favorite movie, but I offend her when I don't like it, when I am not impressed with her collection of memorabilia. I live an hour from the beach, but I don't ever go. I presume it will always be there. Her hurt is a cloak in which she is swallowed. Rage and the lilting language of betrayal spill from her. We had visions we'd be elsewhere, happier, fuller people—there is no better source of poisonous bondage.

FROM *A HUNDRED AND ONE HILARIOUS KNOCK-KNOCK JOKES*

7.

- Knock-knock.
- Who's there?
- A river.
- A river who?
- A river in which I am kneeling. The water is hot, and pushes my heavy body side to side. I still can't get the rushing sound to drown out the cries. Or clean the ash from the skin's crevices. I have never done anything wrong.

29.

- Knock-knock.
- Who's there?
- The story.
- The story who?
- The story in which the maître-d' cannot seat you and your date. The reservation has been taken by a rich couple. The rich woman wears a dress made of black beads. Her nipples are clearly visible between them. The rich man is sipping an expensive wine from a lipsticked glass. The stain is clear even from the door where you stand.

34.

- Knock-knock.
- Who's there?
- You don't know by now?
- I do. But I didn't want it to be the case. Didn't I tell you I'm no good with funerals? Especially my own. And I can get you the money. Next week. I swear. Isn't the sky a great red tonight? They said it was the forest fires that have claimed thirteen lives so far. Four were firefighters, they said.

42.

- Knock-knock.
- Who's there?
- A font designer of great renown, come to bestow upon you the most beautiful and heartbreaking collection of alphanumerical characters ever created.
- A font designer of great renown, come to bestow upon me the most beautiful and heartbreaking collection of alphanumerical characters ever created who?
- The weather is cold. The instructions are all here, in my briefcase. This might be the text that could end all wars. But it might also be the text that could end all desire to go on living. I'm willing to take the chance. Please, let me in. You must be a part of this.

51.

- Knock-knock.
- Who's there?
- In the park.
- In the park who?
- In the park there is a festival at which six thousand red helium balloons are gathered and set free at the same time. Something having to do with peace or disease. In the bushes two high school kids do it for the first time. Some awkward groping. The requisite joke of how long it takes or doesn't take. Depends on the point of view. But the blood rushes to their heads. Great heated vessels open on their faces. Like a daytime sky that is suddenly red with balloons. Or red with fire.

68.

- Knock-knock.
- Who's there?
- Orange.
- Orange who?
- Orange you glad we live in a society of cheap trinkets?
It's not a bad thing at all to be shown this kind of love.

78.

- Knock-knock.
- Who's there?
- The latest news.
- The latest news who?
- The latest news claims it is impossible to write a story without mentioning fire. Or that the fire has already in some way touched your story. The edges burned. But not visibly. It was the first great innovation. Now the flames have licked all our lives, and all our fictions. You've already failed. Don't feel ashamed. None of us is truly an animal no matter how we cower.

80.

- Knock-knock.
- Who's there?
- Your heart.
- Look, I told you that guy moved away. You don't need to keep coming back here like this. Our home is full of love. Full of love's decorations. The photographs in carefully chosen frames. The dirty dishes. Towels. Our underwear thrown over the office chairs in a moment of great heat, of great instability of logic and thought in which the animal took over, in which we suddenly were thrust into a moment of teeth and blackness to awake later satisfied with tears on our lips. We assumed they were of joy.

93.

- Knock-knock.
- Who's there?
- The longest guitar solo.
- The longest guitar solo who?
- The longest guitar solo that ends on the album with what seems like the drummer's death. Suddenly you can hear the cymbal crash to the floor. The guitarist stops and shouts in great alarm "Mike!" But there isn't a response because the record at this point has ended. This was the gift your sister gave you. It terrifies you every time you play it, but you feel you must. You feel it is your duty to pay your respects in this terrible manner.

101.

- Knock-knock.
- Who's there?
- The police.
- The police who?
- The police who have come to tell you that you must evacuate your homes. The fire, the great fire that has blackened the sky of the entire state is almost at your doorstep. You will be killed. You will all be killed.
- We won't leave. Our home is full of love. Full of the decorations of love. Full of heat. Our letters that have been saved. All the greatest alphanumerical characters. Photographs of famous rivers. Full of our soaps. Full of flyers for park festivals. The ones we attended and the ones we meant to attend. Full of trinkets. It was never a bad thing to be loved in that way. Full of collections. Full of our dreams. Full of doors made from beads. Black beads. Full of films that detail the greatest mafia capers ever captured on celluloid and ones that perhaps weren't as good. Full of records given to us by dead relatives. Full of animals other than ourselves. A canary not yet dead. Cats. Two of them. One is pregnant. The other begs for food until we cannot sleep. It would be the greatest honor to die among all of this. Join us. Please. You must be a part of this.

ENOLA GAY

My girlfriend and I saw the plane when it was on display in the Smithsonian. It was just me and Becky, who was Korean. I mean, her family. She could barely even speak it. Just hello, goodbye, love, and grandfather. Anyway, I was a big buff on World War II planes. My favorite was the P-51 Mustang, although I was also partial to the Grumman F6F Hellcat. It was blockier, and the Navy planes weren't as agile, but I always kind of liked the squarish cockpit. The Cadillac of fighter planes. Becky liked it when I got enthusiastic about these things so when she heard about this Hiroshima anniversary exhibit in DC she bought us tickets. I didn't like bombers too much, but *Enola Gay* was *the* bomber, the big one. The most famous warplane that probably ever flew, next to the Red Baron's triplane. We went and just kind of stood there, staring at it in awe, reading all the information about Japanese casualties. The immediate incinerations, the radiation burns. There were radiation deaths caused by the blast all the way up into the early 1990s. This old white man was standing next to us and must have seen us standing mouths agape because he moved right next to us both.

"They were going to nuke Tokyo, you know," he said in a low voice. "Nuke all the damn nips to cinders. Truman said there would be a rain of ruin from the air the likes of which has never been seen on this earth."

Then he looked at us like we were supposed to know what to say, but we had just read the same placards he did. We saw the same quotes. He looked at me and then Becky and walked away. Later, Becky was a little mad at me.

"You should have said something," she said. "He looked like he wanted to bayonet me."

"He was just an old man," I said. "What if I said 'go fuck yourself' and then gave him a heart attack? I wonder if he was a pilot."

Becky wasn't very good at communicating her anger. She acted the rest of the trip like I slept with her sister. We're from San Francisco and didn't deal with this sort of hatred that much, and it bothered me in a bad way. Like I was doing something wrong by dating her. Not to mention she wasn't even Japanese. A hundred thousand people died in Hiroshima. Nagasaki is like an afterthought. The plane *Bockscar* dropped a bomb that killed seventy-five thousand people instantly. I just wanted to appreciate the mechanics of death. The sleekness of these machines. The cute paintings on the side and designs and kitschy names. Maybe that man did too but found it impossible. Somehow guilt stabs its way in everywhere, where the flesh is weak, when you least desire.

MEASURE FOR MEASURE

A list of the dead. A man on the phone. A reason for madness. A cup all emptied. A ghost in the doorway. A river of blood. A flotation device has deployed. A creature needs me. A wallet of bills. A rose by any other name. A case has been reopened. A story of mechanics. A history in pictures. A load of genuine garbage. A beginning with no end. A sky opening up. A tale of several cities. A found notebook. A connection has been lost. A sea of stones. A wedlock of doom. A getaway car is refueled. A victim breaks free. A mouse in the attic. A ghost in the doorway. A question of love. A broken coffeepot. A hole opens up. A river of stones. A wind-carried scream. A joy and a fear. A road leads us nowhere. A tile all cracked up. A catastrophe averted. A ghost in the doorway. A dandelion all pressed. A real true thing.

THE TEMPEST

I thought it wasn't happening but it was. To every girl I thought looked chaste. Chaste, as though that was a compliment. To get to know every blemish of another's body. All the filth, all the little corners. I looked at girls around me and thought they must not want it. I must not want it. They were bearing down on me, I tell you, I tell you, I wanted it. A girl had to change and I hovered in her room for a second, unsure if I should stand out in the hall, if she wanted me to see. She said go stand in the hall. A month later she put my hand on her breast as we stood in front of the mirror. Her grandfather would be home soon. I wanted it. We called many girls tricks. There was always a push in the air. At any second we could break into orgy. We were told we shouldn't want it, that girls especially shouldn't want it. The Lord was everywhere He shouldn't be—the filth we folded within us, the filth we spoke, in our corners. Our filthy broken bread. The sheets. The hot breaths between us were like a sticky film. They ran through the whole school, the whole town. We all wanted it, oh Lord, I couldn't believe it. We wanted and wanted and nothing came.

BILLBOARD

A close friend of mine, a local model, was killed in a highway pileup after a semi-truck jackknifed in rush hour traffic and knocked three cars into the guard rail. I had to help claim her body, and it was the first time I'd ever seen a human being in that state, death with medicinal, cleaned gashes. No blood. I couldn't sleep for days with the strange mesh of fear and grief wrapping itself around my face, my chest. I started taking the bus to work so I wouldn't have to drive anymore. A few months after my friend's death, a new billboard went up along the bus route that I take. It was my friend, her arms folded over her chest, a wry grin on her face, with the words "Get Tested For HPV Today!" and a number to call. When I first saw it I didn't recognize her face, wasn't expecting it in any other context from mourning or grief. Then I became furious, like it was a cruel joke. I called the number on the billboard, and the woman who answered understood my sadness but said she just set up the appointments for testing, and that I should set up an appointment since it was the most commonly transmitted STI in the United States and some strains can lead to an increased risk of cervical cancer. I called my friend's dad, who told me the ad agency's name but said my friend knew about the campaign and was proud of the gig, and the money she had made from it was helping allay the costs of the funeral and burial. That's not why my friend did it though, to pay for her own funeral. She wouldn't have even considered that a possibility. I had to keep seeing her face on my way to work, suddenly emerging from fog to smirk down at me on the bus as I drowned in the severed voices of a podcast about American cakes. I couldn't take another way to work because I still wasn't over my fear of driving and felt I may never be. My friend, she wasn't doing anything wrong, just trying to make it in whatever weird way we have to make it. An HPV billboard is a paying gig, and it might actually help people, but she didn't want it to be her grotesque tombstone, she wanted it to be a funny story she'd tell people decades later. Can-you-believe-it type stuff. Look what I had to do for my craft. The echo of the orchestra's last furious note when the conductor cuts them off. My friend's father said I was making the tragedy about me, by calling in tears, in anger, but that's not my fault. The whole world is about me. It is for all of us.

FESTIVAL OF LIGHTS

A house on Oak St. burned down. We took many photos of it going up in flames at lunchtime, and it was only later, after posting the photos online for comments from friends and strangers, that we found out it was a murder-suicide. We thought it was just that the houses in our neighborhood are old, have bad wiring, careless landlords. We thought it was college kids leaving the burner on, but it was a guy who came home and stabbed his girlfriend nineteen times, then burned the place down to kill himself. He was taken out alive—we got a picture of the stretcher and firemen—but he died due to smoke inhalation that night. We were sad, but we didn't know them, they lived a couple blocks away. A house on Merrill burned down next. The family was away, and the police said it was definitely not electrical. Maybe it was insurance fraud, or maybe it was lightning. Our neighborhood gets the most lightning strikes in the whole county. A house on Davis burned down the very next day, and the police were quiet about the cause. The reporters asked questions, and the police said in front of cameras "No questions." Then, breaking news that a house on Vine was aflame amidst the holiday lights festival. We don't fear fire, though we do not like to be burned. At night, we hear the house shifting, the noise of drunken neighbors stumbling from their cars, and if fear spreads its palms at the inside of our stomach, it's only for the idea of break-ins, ghosts, or that a friend has stumbled to our porch in direst need. We hope our home does not burn down next, today or tomorrow, but we are not scared. Houses keep burning down. We know they are unrelated, but we also know that there is potential for all the houses to burn down at once, unrelatedly. At night, when our neighbors aren't at home, didn't leave on their porch lights, we imagine we live on an island, isolated, we are the only light or heat for a thousand miles. If we step outside, we drown. We die like powder in flame.

ACKNOWLEDGMENTS

The following pieces previously appeared in various forms in the places indicated:

apt – "Paper Dolls"
Artifice Magazine – "Carnivalia"
The Collagist – "Body in the Dumpster,"
        "Disfigurement," "Historical Society"
Denver Quarterly – "Enterprise"
DIAGRAM – "Coriolanus," "Shoebox Bomb," "Tallest
        Person/Shortest Person"
Event – "Choose Your Own Adventure"
Ghost Town Review – "King Lear"
Gold Wake Live – "Two Actors," "The Future Suicides"
Harpur Palate – "Audio Cassette Bought From Goodwill
        Marked 'Kelly'"
Hobart – "Milk"
Inch – "Degrees"
Juked – "Clown, with Maggots in Mouth," "Measure for
        Measure"
Madcap Review – "Hamlet"
Matador Review - "Billboard," "Stitches"
matchbook – "Water in its Three Forms"
Midway Journal - "Wading"
Mizna – "The Color Bearers of the Spring Parade,"
        "Gold Halos"
NOO Journal – "Civilization"
Paper Darts – "Nice Twitter"
Passages North – "Witness Protection"
Ping Pong – "Collapsibility"
Pleiades – "Macbeth"
The Portland Review – "Festival of Lights"
Redivider – "Celeste Celeste," "False Teeth"
RHINO – "From *A Hundred And One Hilarious Knock-
        Knock Jokes*"

SmokeLong Quarterly – "Interference," "The Drone"
Spork – "Infinite Palace," "The Tempest"
Timber – "The Cape Breton Screaming Eagles"
Word Riot – "Enola Gay"

*

Many thanks to the following friends and mentors who've helped me understand prose a little better along the way:

Peter Blickle, Karen Brennan, Andrew Brininstool, Hayan Charara, Franklin KR Cline, Danielle Evans, Jeremy Farnell, Nick Flynn, Jaimy Gordon, Bryan Grosnick, Caitlin Horrocks, Randa Jarrar, Kirby Johnson, Mat Johnson, T. Geronimo Johnson, W. Todd Kaneko, Irene Keliher, Rachel Kincaid, Brandon Krieg, Cadence Kidwell, Matt Killian, Lisa Lee, Jeremy Llorence, Johnathan MacEachern, Oindrila Mukherjee, Colleen O'Brien, Michael Powers, Elizabeth Stuckey-French, and Russel Swensen.

So much gratitude to Kyle and Nick and everyone at Gold Wake for publishing this book on their amazing press.

Much love to my family.

And Laurie, you are my perfect wonder.

ABOUT GOLD WAKE PRESS

Gold Wake Press, an independent publisher, is curated by Nick Courtright and Kyle McCord. All Gold Wake titles are available at Amazon, barnesandnoble.com, and via order from your local bookstore. Learn more at goldwake.com.

Available Titles:

ABOUT THE AUTHOR

Glenn Shaheen is the author of the poetry collection *Predatory* (University of Pittsburgh Press, 2011), winner of the Agnes Lynch Starrett Poetry Prize and runner-up for the Norma Farber First Book Award; the flash fiction chapbook *Unchecked Savagery* (Ricochet Editions, 2013); and the poetry collection *Energy Corridor* (University of Pittsburgh Press, 2016).

CPSIA information can be obtained
at www.ICGtesting.com
Printed in the USA
BVHW03s1827270218
509243BV00001B/40/P